n the beginning . . .

Martha was Helen's dog. She was an ordinary dog until . . .

. . . the day she ate alphabet soup.

The letters in the soup traveled up to her brain instead of down to her stomach.

That night Martha spoke:

When's dinner?

ve you heard th?
e about the ca
walks into a pet
and orders a can
of dog food . . .

Martha just loved to talk.

Steak is at the base of my food pyramid, along with alphabet soup. Above that is just meat in general.

Martha had a lot to tell her family.

Good dog, Skits!

Woof!

And talk . . .

Hello, world! I'm Martha and I'm talking to you!

Is the world ready for Martha?

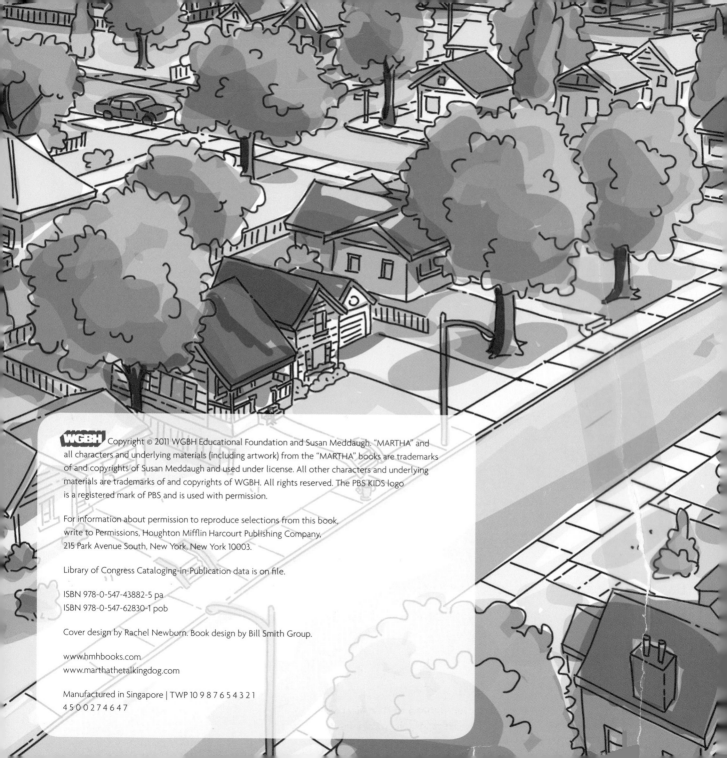

For information about permission to reproduce selections from this book, write to Permissions, Houghton Mifflin Harcourt Publishing Company, 215 Park Avenue South, New York, New York 10003.

Library of Congress Cataloging-in-Publication data is on file.

ISBN 978-0-547-43882-5 pa
ISBN 978-0-547-62830-1 pob

Cover design by Rachel Newborn. Book design by Bill Smith Group.

www.hmhbooks.com
www.marthathetalkingdog.com

Manufactured in Singapore | TWP 10 9 8 7 6 5 4 3 2 1
4 5 0 0 2 7 4 6 4 7

Pool Party

Adaptation by Karen Barss

Based on the TV series teleplay written by Melissa Stephenson and Raye Lankford

Based on the characters created by Susan Meddaugh

Houghton Mifflin Harcourt
Boston • New York • 2011

"This is a great idea, Truman!" said T.D.

Truman had coated playing cards with plastic so they could play games in the pool in his backyard.

"Yes," Helen agreed. "When it's this hot, a pool is the only place I want to be."

Alice rushed into the yard.

"Sorry I'm late," she said. "I had to get a new tube of sunscreen so I wouldn't get sunburned."

Alice slathered her arms, legs, and face with sunscreen.
Then she jumped into the pool with a big splash.

"I put on sunscreen too," Helen said. "It's a good idea."

"My skin is so fair, I burn really easily," said Alice. "I can't take chances, especially since Tiffany's pool party is tomorrow!"

Fur works for me!

The friends climbed out of the pool and ran through the sprinkler. Alice started rubbing sunscreen on her face and arms.

"Uh . . . you just finished doing that," said T.D.

"It might have washed off," Alice said.

Then they played badminton. Alice stopped abruptly to put on more sunscreen.

"Again?" asked Helen.

"I might have sweated it off," replied Alice.

Mine! Mine!

At lunchtime, Alice squeezed more lotion on her arms, legs, and face.

"Don't tell me you ate it off," said Truman.

Alice shrugged. "I'm not the sort of kid who takes chances."

The friends played duck, duck, goose, wearing sunglasses
in the bright sun.

T.D. walked around the circle, "Duck . . . duck . . . duck . . ."
When he got to Alice, he stopped and gasped!
The other kids raised their sunglasses and stared.

"Alice," T.D. said slowly. "You should get out of the sun."

"What? Am I red?" asked Alice.

"Not exactly," T.D. replied. "Sort of a bronzy . . . browny . . . orange."

Alice took off her sunglasses and gasped.

"This is the worst sunburn ever!" And she grabbed her
T-shirt and ran home.

Alice's mother looked at her skin, shaking her head.

"It's not sunburn. It's dye. Like the stuff you use to color Easter eggs," she explained.

"You bought a self-tanning suncreen by mistake," her mother said. "It has a chemical that dyes your skin."

"But who would want to be dyed orange?" Alice asked.

"I think that only happens if you use too much," her mother replied.

"I have to get this off!" Alice said later that afternoon. "I can't go to Tiffany's pool party looking like an orange Easter egg!"

"I have an idea," T.D. said.

"Me too," said Truman.

And they both left.

Truman returned with a jar.

"I brought you some of my mom's body scrub. It says, 'Removes old skin and produces a fresh, dewy glow in minutes.' "

Alice grabbed the jar and scrubbed. But she was still orange.

T.D. appeared with a bowl of lemon wedges.

"My Grandma says lemons fade freckles," he explained.

Alice rubbed her arms and legs. "They aren't helping, are they?"

T.D. shook his head. "No . . . but you smell zesty!"

When the friends left Alice's house, they were disappointed.

"Alice can't miss Tiffany's pool party," said Helen. "It's going to be the best party ever!"

Suddenly, Martha perked up. "I have an idea," she said.

She whispered something to Helen. "I like it," said Helen, smiling.

Martha ran to all her friends' houses and then returned home.
"I told everyone I could think of," she reported to Helen.
"Do you think they'll do it?" Helen asked.
"Of course they will," Martha replied. "Who could refuse a talking dog?"

The next morning, Alice sat on her bed—hot, discouraged, and orange.

"Helen called to say she found a way for you to blend in," Alice's mom said.

"But Mom, I look like a gumdrop with glasses!" Alice replied.

"Just go. You'll have fun."

Alice grabbed a towel and left to change into her bathing suit, feet dragging.

At Tiffany's house, Alice reluctantly opened the gate.
She couldn't believe her eyes!

"Well? What do you think?" asked Martha, wagging her orange tail.

"We didn't want you to feel self-conscious about being orange," Helen explained.

Alice threw her arms around her friends.
"I have the best friends ever!" she said.

And they all jumped into the pool with a splash!